LUMBER JILLS

THE UNSUNG HEROINES OF WORLD WAR II

Alexandra Davis

illustrated by
Katie Hickey

Albert Whitman & Company
Chicago, Illinois

Author's Note

The stories recounted by individual Lumber Jills are as varied as the girls themselves. But there are two constant themes sparkling through them all: the girls' deep friendship with one another and the cheerful determination with which they worked. Individually, each girl believed she could make a difference to the fate of the world, one small action at a time. And collectively, that's just what they did.

And while this story takes place with World War II as the backdrop, it is not really a war story. It's a heroes' story meant for our children—the universally small—as an encouragement and reminder that even the very small can change the course of history. All they need to do is show up with willing hands and stout hearts.

I dedicate this to the young women who became Lumber Jills—
may your courage, sacrifice, and cheerfulness inspire us all.
Thank you for your service.
To my husband, Daniel, and my son, Gideon; I adore you both.—AD

For my grandmothers, Sylvia and Patricia—KH

Library of Congress Cataloging-in-Publication data is on file with the publisher.

Text copyright © 2019 by Alexandra Davis
Illustrations copyright © 2019 by Katie Hickey
First published in the United States of America in 2019 by Albert Whitman & Company
ISBN 978-0-8075-4795-3

Printed in China
10 9 8 7 6 5 4 3 2 1 NP 22 21 20 19

Design by Ellen Kokontis

For more information about Albert Whitman & Company,
visit our website at www.albertwhitman.com.

100 Years of Albert Whitman & Company
Celebrate with us in 2019!

One pair of woolen socks pulled up to the knee.

Two loving parents smile and kiss their girl goodbye.
Four sturdy brown boots running down the road.
Sixteen train cars chugging up the tracks.

Twenty-seven new girls signing up to serve, with two hands willing to work and one stout heart.

One pair of woolen socks pulled up to the knee.

Eight blankets folded neatly make it feel like home.

Two hundred cheerful girls learn to cut the trees.
Four hundred gum boots muddle through the mud.
Two hands willing to work and one stout heart.

One pair of woolen socks pulled up to the knee.

Two girls to chop and saw and split one giant tree.

One girl measures well, another leads the team.

One cart is loaded high and moving to the mill.

Six painful blisters heal and strengthen over time.
Two hands willing to work and one stout heart.

One pair of woolen socks pulled up to the knee.
One sweater, soft and green, warms against the chill.
Three girls burn the brush, as well as warm the tea.

Four hundred girls sing while they walk to camp.

Five nights are spent indoors, writing letters home.
Two games are all they have; they play them till they're bored.

Two hands willing to work and one stout heart.

One pair of woolen socks pulled up to the knee.
One coat, big and brown, for working in the snow.

Four o'clock, the sun is down and all must leave the woods.
Four miles down the lanes until they reach the light...

One dance hall, brightly lit; the band plays loud and clear.
Ten shades of lipstick red smile big and bright.

Forty-seven service men are at the weekend dance.

Two hands willing to hold and one stout heart.

One pair of woolen socks pulled up to the knee.
Two thousand Lumber Jills singing "Timber-HO!"

Ten million trees cut and sent into the war.

As telegraph poles and roadblocks and pitprops and more.
As warships and fast trains and airplanes galore.

As wood for trucks and wood for crates.
Wood for fences, wood for gates.

Ten million trees cut and sent into the world
for those at home and those away,

that faith and hope would light the way.

Two hands willing to work and one stout heart.

One pair of woolen socks pulled up to the knee.

Sixteen train cars chugging up the tracks.

Four faithful brown boots coming down the road.
Two loving parents wave and kiss their girl hello.

Twenty-seven good friends singing the same song, of
two hands willing to work and one stout heart.

About the Lumber Jills

During World War II, 8,500 British girls joined the little-known Women's Timber Corps. They were armed with nothing but four-and-a-half-pound axes, six-pound saws, and the willingness to pick them up. The average Lumber Jill was eighteen years old, and while these girls came from all walks of life, most of them had never lifted an axe before. In spite of this, they were not judged by their size or strength but by their enthusiasm, resilience, and good humor.

They received one month of training in felling (chopping a tree down), snedding (removing the bark and small branches), cross-cutting (cutting a tree into logs), and measuring. After training they moved to forests all over England and Scotland to begin their work in earnest. The girls tackled the challenges of living in primitive conditions—without heat, electricity, or hot water—with plucky determination. As more lumberjacks were called to war, the Lumber Jills learned harder and more specialized roles, becoming skilled horsewomen, haulers, truck drivers, and sawmill operators.

It's hard to fathom the breadth and depth to which the success of the war depended on the Lumber Jills and the trees they cut down. One small example: Without the Lumber Jills' pitprops in coal mines, coal production would have stopped within the first seven months of the war. Without coal, the country couldn't produce steel, which was used to make tanks, ships, submarines, and airplanes. Without coal, families couldn't heat their homes.

As it turns out, the story of the Lumber Jills is an American and Canadian one too. There are stories of women working alongside lumberjacks long before World War II, and when the war came, women confidently marched into the woods to "do their part." Across North America an estimated eighty thousand women worked in the timber industry during the war years—from New Hampshire, where thirteen women ran an all women's sawmill, to the South, where women took over the paper mills, to the Pacific Northwest, where they worked every aspect of the timber and forestry cycle. In British Columbia there was a timber town whose labor force was 80 percent women at the height of the war.

Though divided by an ocean, the British, American, and Canadian girls who became Lumber Jills were unified by their mission and made cheerful by their abiding friendships.